Mojo's Story

By

Margaret Gray

Mojo's Story

ISBN : 9781521238219

Mojo's Story

Acknowledgements

With thanks to Ellen, Phil, Mojo, Wiggle and Arthur
for inspiring this story.

Table of Contents

Mojo's Story

Chapter 1

The Meeting

I could hear them coming. My heart started pounding and I trembled from nose to tail. I crouched beside the bronzed bracken. Should I throw myself on their mercy or should I try to get through another winter in the wild? My aching joints and muscles helped me make my decision.

The humans were chatting happily and I was reassured by their voices. This was my chance but I had better not spook their horses. I rose and slowly pushed myself through the undergrowth. I whined as I limped along the edge of the rough track. I glanced mournfully up at the humans. Had they spotted me? Would they stop?

I thought I had approached gently enough but one of the horses was rearing and snorting. Fortunately, the man brought it under control quickly. He dismounted and talked soothingly to the jittery horse. I whined again and the man handed the horse's reins to the woman. I slumped to the ground and chewed at my sore right paw.

The man approached cautiously but I had no intension of biting him. I whimpered as I studied him. He looked tanned and fit. His shoulder-length, grey hair was tied back and his voice was deep and gentle. He knelt beside me and picked up my injured paw.

The woman was now standing alongside, holding the reins of both horses. She was slim and pretty. Normally, she had an easy smile but now she looked concerned. As she pushed back her hair, which was the colour of the rising sun, the woman said "I think this is the dog that has been hanging around recently." The horses sniffed at me before starting to graze on the meagre scrub. They could see that I was not a threat after all.

"It's a scruffy beast so I don't think she's anyone's pet. There's a thorn embedded deep between her toes. Can you hold the paw firmly while I try to ease it out please, Helen?"

I yelped as they worked together to draw the thorn out. "It looks as though it's been here for a while. The whole area is inflamed. Have you got any water left?"

The woman put my paw down while she pulled a bottle of liquid from her saddlebag. She poured water over my sore pad and toes before the pair started to work on the thorn again. I was beginning to regret their attention when they eventually managed to extract the woody spike.

She emptied the bottle of water over the wound. I lapped up the excess water and licked the tender area. Yes. If my instincts were right, these humans would make excellent companions.

They remounted their horses and headed back towards their yard. I checked that my right paw could take my weight and then followed them at a discreet distance. The woman released both horses in their field while the man filled buckets with oats and food pellets, which he carried to the field and placed on the ground in front of the horses.

I leapt forward, knocking over one of the buckets. I started gulping down the food pellets before the horses could get close. The man shouted at me and waved his arms but I was famished and stood my ground.

He shared the remaining contents of the buckets between the two horses. The humans held the buckets out for the horses so that I could not steal any more pellets. Then they strapped turnout rugs over the animals to keep them warm.

I followed the humans back to their yard where they hung up the riding tack. I sat beside a big bag of food pellets, looking from the face of the woman back to the man. They laughed and put containers of food and water at the end of the lane for me.

I spent the night beside a wooden building in the lane, thinking about how I could train them properly. I needed more than food to make my life more comfortable.

This was the second leaf-fall period that I had been living in the wild, scrounging edibles from humans and hunting. I had seen other dogs with their companions. Life seemed easy for most of them.

Generally, they appeared healthy and well fed, sometimes a little too well fed, if you ask me. They could spend time playing with their human friends because they did not need to hunt for enough food to survive. I would like to try that lifestyle now. Puppyhood has been harsh.

As I dozed off, my memories flitted through my mind.

Chapter 2

Puppyhood

I was born in the forest after my mother had been abandoned there. She did her best to feed her puppies but she was living on meagre handouts and scraps. We were underfed.

Sometimes mother discovered kennels and outhouses where bowls of food and water were left outside for working dogs. She would gobble down as much as she could before any other creatures could take it. Her milk was richer and more plentiful at those times and we felt less hungry.

Quite often, it was several days before our presence was noticed by any humans. Then we would have things thrown at us, to scare us away. Generally, the working dogs themselves seemed to tolerate us but some were vicious and noisy. Mother would then herd us away to save us from attacks.

I was happiest when mother took us to buildings where humans ate and drank outside. She would push us forward for people to make a fuss of us. Mother would let us play rough and tumble at those places and it seemed to amuse everyone. We were even allowed to play with the dogs that belonged to the humans. Most people would throw down food for mother when they saw how thin and ragged she looked.

We were never allowed inside the buildings and they closed down during the darkness. It was good if there were barns or sheltered yards nearby where we could sleep safely.

Although mother would suckle us as often as she could, she was not getting the right food. Normally, she was unable to produce enough milk to feed us all and most of my brothers and sisters died, one by one.

Mother managed to struggle along and she was able to keep me and my elder brother alive. That was until she became very poorly. We did not know what had happened but she developed a nasty red patch on her chest. Then an oozing ulcer appeared and she started being very sick and tired. She could no longer feed us at all and within a few days she too died. We sat beside her lifeless body all day, whining and moping, nudging her occasionally to try to stir her back into life.

My brother and I suddenly found ourselves on our own, not knowing how to look after ourselves. We were thirsty and very hungry indeed. What were we to do?

My brother started padding along a path, drawn towards bright shafts of sunlight. He stopped every so often to sniff the air. I followed him and then I too noticed a lovely smell of food. Before long, we found ourselves outside one of our favourite places.

There were no humans around but we found a bowl that we had seen mother lapping from on our last visit. So we did the same. Then we walked round the building and found another bowl. We kept sniffing the air. The aroma was really strong now but it seemed to be coming from inside the building and we could not see an obvious way in. We sat outside a doorway that we had seen humans use to get inside the building.

We waited for what seemed like a long time but no one came out. So my brother put his head back and howled. I copied him. That did the trick. We soon heard the sounds of movement and the door was pushed open. We moved forward cautiously and looked up at the man in the doorway. He seemed to recognise us and looked around for our mother. He pointed a finger at us and in a strong, commanding voice said “Sit. Wait.” Then he shut the door in our faces and disappeared.

My brother and I looked at each other. What would happen now? We waited and before long the man reappeared. He put a bowl in front of each of us. The bowls both contained a couple of strips of the lovely smelling meat. The man closed the door on us while we chewed on the salty treat. We were so hungry that the food lasted no time at all and we wanted more.

The man seemed in no hurry to return so we started howling again. Eventually, he returned. Bringing a finger up towards his lips, he shouted “Stop! Shush!” and tossed a large bone away from the door. We tumbled over each other as we rushed to see what he had thrown for us. The bone had quite a lot of pink flesh on it. It smelt different from what we had just eaten but the scent was pleasant, so we tried eating the meat.

Our little teeth just combed through the flesh at first and the bone itself was much too big and hard for us to bite into. We were starving so we had to try and eat this somehow. My brother crouched down at one of the knobbly ends of the bone and crossed his paws over it. I did the same, at the other end, and we found that we could tear small mouthfuls of meat off the bone by twisting our jaws.

I felt much better. I closed my eyes as I chewed on the meal in front of me. Every so often, my brother would tug the bone closer to himself but I just pulled it back. We must share if we were to survive. When we had finished the meat, we started gnawing on the bone. Finally, we licked it over and over until we were certain there was nothing left. We fell asleep alongside our first bone.

We were rudely awoken when our prize was snatched from our grasp by a large, bracken-coloured dog. He growled fiercely at us and the fur on the back of his neck rose into a stiff ridge. I cowered. I was not going to fight him for a dry bone. My brother yapped in annoyance but did not confront the dog. We slunk off to find some water to drink.

With our noses close to the ground, we sniffed all around the building. We checked every nook and cranny in the hope of finding something to eat. We chewed anything that looked or smelt like food and soon learned to ignore foul-tasting, white or bracken-coloured tubes. These were the remains of what the humans put in their mouths to make choking smoke. We found very little, so settled down by the doorway and dozed.

We woke to the sound of crunching on the gravel area close to the building. Humans had started to arrive and the glorious smell of food wafted around us. We pranced towards the humans, tails wagging. They made a fuss of us but did not feed us. However, the man who had fed us earlier did put some more water out for us. We felt cheated when other dogs started drinking ***our*** water.

We felt better when some young humans came and played rough and tumble with us. They threw things for us, yelling “Fetch!”. A man sat close by to watch our frolics.

Then he opened a crackling packet and threw a few roundish things on the ground close to us. The roundels smelt nice but broke into small pieces when we tried to eat them. The bits tasted good and we sat at the man’s feet, hoping for more. The young humans cried “Can we have some crisps to feed to the puppies, please, Daddy?” We were reminded of the happy times with our mother. Now, however, we would have to rely on humans like these to feed us.

All too soon, the family left but we quickly found some more small people to play with. My brother and I were exhausted but happy by the time the building was closed up and the humans had all drifted away. We flopped down by the doorway again and closed our eyes.

My brother woke me up with his howling. I could hear and smell the man who had given us the bone earlier. He was opening the door. Hopefully, he had more food for us. However, he waved his arms about and yelled “Clear off!”

I thought he was playing with us at first but when he threw some gravel, which hit me on the rump, I knew he did not want us around. We padded away a short distance and then looked back at the man again, just in case he was teasing us. No. He shouted and picked up more gravel. My brother yelped as a sharp stone hit his back. We fled.

Just when I thought we had found a way to survive, my hopes were dashed. Feeling dejected, we waddled into the woods. A group of ponies was grazing so we sniffed around their hooves to find out if we could beat them to any morsels. They were just cropping the grass, which did not taste very nice at all. In fact, it nearly made me sick.

While I was retching, one of the ponies kicked me and I fell into a muddy ditch. Frantically, I struggled to clamber up the steep sides. My brother grabbed the fold of skin round my neck and tugged me out. I felt very sorry for myself. I was sore and hungry and I stank.

After a brief rest, we toddled along a well-worn path. I tried to remember what our mother used to eat. With my nose close to the ground, I searched for something that smelt like food. However, the reek of my fur masked all other smells.

We emerged from the wooded area onto the heath. I saw a pool of water and, instinctively, started paddling in it. I rolled around at the water's edge until I could no longer smell the caked mud. We took a drink before wandering on, aimlessly now.

The water had taken the edge off our hunger but we needed to eat something soon. I recalled mother chasing feathery creatures when they landed on the ground or furry animals that came out of their holes to nibble on the grass. Those were what we needed to look out for.

My weariness got the better of me and I sank down onto a patch of lush grass. I put my head on my front paws and let out a deep sigh. My side ached where the pony had kicked me. My brother had no time for self pity and he carried on over the heath, looking for prey.

I heard a gentle, snuffling sound and opened my eyes to look directly at a furry animal, similar to those that mother used to chase. I blinked in disbelief but otherwise kept still. I had spotted my brother sneaking up behind the creature in the hope of pouncing on it.

My brother sprang and landed squarely on the creature's back. It tried to wriggle away but I leapt forward, forgetting my woes. Between us, we managed to overpower our victim. We could not believe it.

Now we could eat. At first, we simply bit into mouthfuls of dry, choking fur. Then my brother found a soft bit of flesh under the fur and pulled the pelt back so that we could eat the rich meat underneath.

We were very exposed on that open patch so, between us, we wrestled the limp body into the nearby undergrowth. We tucked into our first kill. It was fortunate that my brother had decided to come back and urge me onwards.

We ate until we were full and then my brother left me on guard while he found somewhere to stash the remains of our carcass. We dragged it under some old tree roots and spent the night, snuggling together, with our heads resting on the soft fur.

Having stretched our aching limbs the next morning, we tucked into the remains of our catch. Now we had the energy to chase each other round the tree and up and down the slope alongside the tree roots.

Our efforts left us panting and thirsty so we went in search of another pool. We splashed and played before lying down at the water's edge, enjoying the warmth of the sun on our black backs. Life felt good again.

It was time to look for our next meal. We watched for signs of movement on the heath and pointed our noses towards the sky, breathing in the scent-laden air. We toddled towards the most promising area. Another furry animal, like the one we were lucky enough to capture the previous day, would suit us nicely.

We passed many strange, flitting and buzzing creatures as we wandered along. I tried catching them but they were usually too quick for me. Some things were very pretty and, as they stayed in one place, I tasted them to see if they were enjoyable.

Nothing we found would make a filling meal. We stopped to play for a while before sniffing the air again. I thought I could smell humans so it was worth heading in that direction. We frolicked along a promising track.

Eventually, we came across another building with wooden tables and seats outside. A short-legged pony was munching on something around the seats. I had never seen such a small pony and thought it might want to play. So I pranced up to it but it just snorted and carried on grazing. Its legs were very sturdy and I did not want to be kicked again.

My brother and I snuffled around for food too, keeping clear of the pony's hooves. Before long, some humans did appear so we approached them in the hope of titbits. A man shook a packet of crisps at me so I put my front paws on his knee. He opened the bag and held it above my head. I tried to stand on my hind legs but kept tumbling over. I yapped in frustration.

However, my brother jumped up onto the seat and snatched the packet out of the man's hand. The man shouted at him in surprise but then laughed as we tucked into the crisp pieces. Another human scattered the contents of a different packet on the ground in front of us and we scoffed the lot in seconds. We approached all the humans and begged for food.

Suddenly, we were surrounded by lovely smells. People started carrying plates from the building. The plates were loaded with meals and were put on the tables in front of the seated humans.

We did not know where to turn. We went to the people who had already made a fuss of us. We quickly learned that the best way of getting handouts was to sit beside someone and keep looking from face to plate and back again. Add a whimper and a paw on the knee and we could not fail.

By the time the building had closed and the people had left, we were full. We settled down under a table and went to sleep. It had been a good morning.

When we woke up, we were thirsty so hunted for some water containers. There were several wedged in corners around the building. My brother found a soft, round ball alongside one of the bowls. It smelt of other dogs.

He picked it up in his jaws and dropped it, as he had seen other dogs do. It just stopped still in the leaf-strewn grass. So I grabbed it from under his nose and scampered away with it. He gave chase and we tumbled over each other.

I dropped the ball and it rolled away this time because we were now on a slope. My brother caught the ball before it reached the bottom of the slope. He scrambled back up the bank and dropped the ball again. This time, I chased it. We played like that until we were too weary to carry on.

Then it started to rain so we sheltered under the eaves of the building, waiting for the humans to return. It seemed a long time before any arrived. They went into the building but mainly stayed inside. The only people we saw were those with smelly, white sticks in their mouths. We tried to avoid the white clouds that they blew out of their mouths.

No one came out into the rain with any food for us. So we started howling and yapping. One of the cloud-blowers came out and ran at us to chase us away. We thought it was a game until he started throwing stones at us.

By now, the rain was getting heavier and the wind was strong and gusty. We slunk off round the building to find shelter, away from the angry man. There were several wooden buildings close by but we could not find a way into any of them. We found one spot where we could lie right alongside one wall of the main building. We were just out of the rain there and that was where we spent a cool, draughty night.

We felt miserable as the darkness lifted. It was still cold, wet and windy. We shook briskly to clear the rain off our fur and had a play-fight to warm up. Feeling a little more cheerful, we wandered round the buildings again in the hope of finding food.

However, we were out of luck. Dare we risk calling for attention? We had to try. There was no response. We could not even smell anything tasty. So we headed back onto the heath. Perhaps we could catch another furry animal.

A black, feathery creature was digging its sharp, pointed nose into the grass. We stopped in our tracks and sank down, getting as close to the earth as we could. We could try and catch the glossy bird before it leapt into the air above us. If we missed it, we might be able to eat whatever it was hunting for.

However, we had been spotted and with a harsh "Caah!" the crow lifted off the ground, effortlessly, and drifted away towards the woodland. We nosed around the grass where it had been searching but there was nothing worth eating.

We toddled on until we too were on the edge of the tree line. We spotted a pair of birds that had not noticed us. They were more interested in each other. That might be our chance.

My brother started creeping away to the side to try and get into the woodland behind the birds. I crouched down, barely moving. I could feel my chest thumping but the courting creatures did not seem to hear.

As my brother slowly rose up behind the birds, I sprang forward. Between us, we managed to catch the larger bird. Its lovely, long feathers flew everywhere but we held on to the plump body. The smaller, drab creature scuttled away into the undergrowth.

We tore more feathers off our catch. Some stuck to our muzzles and we started sneezing furiously. We were so hungry that we bit into the flesh as soon as we could see enough to eat. Once we had taken a few mouthfuls, we dragged the limp body into the woodland so that our prize was less likely to be spotted by other hungry creatures.

There was enough meat on the body to provide another meal so we looked around for somewhere to hide it. Just ahead, was a moss-covered tree stump. It was slightly tilted and had a large hole alongside. That would do nicely.

Digging our noses deep into the feathers, we both grabbed a mouthful of flesh and tried hauling the remains of the pheasant towards the tree stump. It was not easy. We kept sneezing as more feathers got up our noses. We tripped over the long, trailing tail and sometimes we were not even pulling in the same direction.

Eventually, we reached the stump and my brother pushed the bird into the hole with his front paws. He left the tail hanging out over the edge of the hole, so we could haul our next meal out again. I would not have thought of that. My brother had obviously been watching our mother's hunting skills carefully. We sank down, panting heavily, and rested.

I was woken by the sound of chattering and snuffling. I looked around and spotted a squirrel searching for food. It was sniffing around the leaves for nutty snacks.

I wondered if I could catch it. However, as I started to turn to face it, the squirrel churred at me and sprang gracefully away. I tried to copy the elegant spring as I moved towards the squirrel but I landed on my rump. The creature clambered briskly up the nearest tree. My poor attempts at following it were met with scornful yakking.

The commotion woke my brother and he came to see what all the noise was about. He yawned and returned to the pheasant by the tree stump. I padded over to join him in the feast. The squirrel was soon forgotten.

My brother again pushed the bird's remains into the hole. Then we gambolled off together to find some water. The woodland and heath were particularly beautiful in that area. There were colourful rhododendron and gorse bushes everywhere. Life felt good at that time.

After a long drink, we splashed about at the water's edge. We tumbled and plunged together but I became scared when I could not feel firm ground under my feet. Thrusting my nose in the air, I moved my legs rapidly backwards and forwards and found that I could keep my head above the water.

In no time, my feet touched the bottom of the pond again and I rushed to get out of the water. I shook myself and sat panting on the muddy grass. My brother was still playing in the pond. He was biting at the eddies he made as he swam in circles.

He soon joined me at the water's edge and we decided we needed more food. We frolicked back towards the remains of our pheasant. However, our stash had been plundered. We followed the scent and trail of feathers into the woodland. Eventually, we were faced with a deep hole. We had never come across some of the strong smells that were coming from the den.

We took turns in cautiously looking into the hole but all we could see was blackness. We yapped at the entrance to the den and peered inside again. That time, we were met with a deep growl that echoed round the hole. We ran away in fright. We would have to find a meal somewhere else.

We were angry that another creature had stolen our food. Feeling dejected, we wandered along a track through the woods. We sniffed the air but everything smelt damp and earthy.

We could not smell any food so we kept moving. Not long before, we had felt so carefree. Our joy had turned to sorrow so quickly. Over time, I learned that this often happened in life.

Without noticing the change in our surroundings, we started to pick up strong smells of other animals again. We stopped and looked around. We were back on the heath and facing a horse-like creature with branches on its head. It was scary to us puppies but we decided to take a closer look anyway.

The beast snorted at us and lifted a front leg. It stamped on the ground so we stopped and watched it. It lifted the same leg again but this time it strode off, jerkily, into the woodland behind. We were impressed by the way it held its head high as it melted away into the background.

Rather than follow the animal, which I later learned was a stag, my brother and I took a well worn path across the heath. Maybe it would take us to an eating place. We kept sniffing the air and started to pick up the familiar aroma of human food.

Yes. Ahead was an old building with a straw roof and there were benches and tables on the closely cropped grass in front of it. We had not seen this place before so, hopefully, we would be given food there.

As we approached a doorway, there was a furry animal dozing in the weak sunshine. Its eyes opened wide in surprise and anger when it smelt and heard us. Then it hissed, stood up and arched its back, hissing again.

Unlike the furry creature we had caught recently, this one showed us an array of sharp, pointed teeth. We would probably have been hurt if we had tried to make a meal of it. The animal sprang towards us and then disappeared round the corner of the building.

I vaguely remembered having seen animals like this before, when our mother was still alive. She called them "Catzzz" or something like that. I suddenly shivered. I had not thought about mother for days. My brother and I had been engrossed in looking for food and seeing so many new things that I had forgotten her. I wished she was still around to help us.

We padded around the building, sniffing out water and titbits. There were only a few dried-up scraps - not enough to stifle our hunger. Returning to the doorway, my brother scratched on the woodwork. There was no response, so he used both paws to claw wildly at the door.

Someone was coming so we stepped back and sat on our haunches. A woman's head appeared at the side of the door. She seemed surprised. We wagged our tails in expectation and yipped gently. She shut the door in our faces and we heard her walk away, muttering loudly.

We waited a while and then barked again, in case the woman had forgotten us. Eventually she returned, scolding us "Hang on a minute, you noisy tykes!" She opened the door, balancing two small dishes of meaty chunks on one of her broad arms.

Waddling down the pathway, with us prancing at her heels, our saviour put the dishes down well away from the entrance to the building. She let out an "Umph!" as she bent down but I did not notice any more until I had licked the bowl clean. The bottom of the bowl grated as it swivelled round and round as I licked. Then we lapped at each other's gravy-covered muzzle and had a play-fight. We settled down in the shade and dozed off.

The next thing I knew, I was being dangled by the scruff of my neck by the broad-armed woman. My brother was in her other hand. We wriggled as much as we could while she marched us to the rear of the building. She kicked a shed door open and shoved us roughly into a corner while she stepped back through the door, closing it behind her. We heard a bolt being drawn across to lock us in.

We whimpered in the dark, confused by our sudden capture. My eyes began to adjust to the dimness and I could see shafts of light streaming between the wooden boards. My brother had also noticed the gaps between the panels. I could see him peering through one of the knot holes. He then started scratching at the knot hole. If he could make a big enough hole, we could escape.

I sniffed around the shed to see if I could find a better escape route. There was a pile of logs in one corner and the floor was covered in sawdust that made me sneeze. I started scrambling up the logs to reach a sunbeam. However, the logs rolled under my feet and I tumbled down into the choking sawdust.

Finding another gap in the planking, I too started scratching, frantically. We clawed and scrabbled until our paws bled. The wood splintered but did not give way. Then we heard the woman shouting as she came nearer the shed. We crouched close to the door, ready to spring when it opened.

The bolt rattled back and the moment there was a chink of daylight, we rushed past our captor. She was knocked sidewise by our headlong plunge through the doorway. I was splashed with the water from a bowl that fell out of her hand but I just kept running. We raced away, not caring where we were going. We just wanted to be out of that place.

Eventually, we came to a halt. I collapsed amongst some bracken, panting rapidly. My chest was heaving and my throat was dry and sore. Steam was rising from our hot bodies. In future, we would stay away from those buildings and rely on each other to find food.

Chapter 3

The Hunters

Our dash for freedom marked the change in our lives from puppies to hunters. We still looked like puppies but, from that day, we rarely had time to play. We stayed away from humans as much as possible. We no longer trusted them.

We did not recognise the area so searched around for some shelter. A large tree had been blown down and its broken trunk and branches provided some cover. Crawling under the trunk, we would be out of much of the wind and rain. That spot would do until we found something better.

After lapping water, greedily and noisily, from a peaty bog amongst the trees, we sniffed the air and walked off in search of food. We followed a leafy path, looking for obvious features that would help us find our way back. My brother cocked his leg against trunks and posts, so that we could return along our own scent tracks.

Coming out of the scrubby thicket, we were faced by a marshy field. We stopped in our tracks and immediately sank to the ground. Ahead of us were a couple of large birds. A chunky, goose was flapping its wings and making little charges towards a tall, grey bird. The heron seemed unmoved by the aggression and strange honking noise coming from the goose.

As my brother slunk off to the right, I inched forward. When we thought we were within striking distance, we leapt towards the goose. My brother caught one of its wings. As it flapped furiously and started spinning round, I sprang onto its back. I sank my teeth into the bird's neck. With a mouth full of feathers, my brother let the wing go and bit into the front of the neck. The bird kept fighting and honking in anger and fear but we managed to hold on until we had choked it.

Suddenly, it was eerily quiet, apart from our panting. The heron had gone. We crouched either side of our prize until we had recovered from the struggle. Together we dragged the carcass back into the scrub land so that we could tackle it away from competition.

Having learned from our earlier pheasant catch, we had less difficulty tackling the heavy bird. Our first few mouthfuls were mainly feathers. However, we noticed that a quick twist of our muzzles, whilst snorting, cleared most of the feathers. Then we could bite into bare skin. We tucked into the feast until we were full. Resting our front paws and heads on the body, which was still warm, we fell asleep.

Heavy rain woke us. We took turns to drink from the marsh, too wary to leave our next meal unguarded. However, we now needed shelter and were too far from the fallen tree to haul our goose. My brother wandered around the area to search for nearby cover. Having found a mound of twigs and branches in the thicket, we pulled the bird to it and hunkered down.

That catch lasted several days and was beginning to get rancid and fly-covered. It was time to look for something different. We decided to check on our previous shelter first, so followed our scent trail away from the woodpile and marshy field.

A brown, spiky creature was crossing a grassy patch in front of us. I had not seen anything like it before. Could we eat it? I touched the animal gingerly with a paw and quickly pulled my leg away. We both sniffed the curiosity and then it rolled up into a prickly ball. It was too big to get our mouths around. The creature really did not look very edible so we left the hedgehog alone and wandered on.

Eventually, we reached the fallen tree and the gap under the broken trunk was still dry and unoccupied. Good, we could return but first we needed to find some food. We set off again, working in wider and wider circles around the tree stump.

We came across a couple of squirrels, rummaging for food. As usual, we froze and watched their movements.

Unfortunately, one of the squirrels was facing us. As soon as it saw us go into stalking mode, it gave a sharp call of alarm. The pair shot away in opposite directions and scrambled up different trees. They screeched at us in anger.

We continued our search for food and found ourselves near a place where people left their cars. We were on the edge of the woodland and heath. A large, beautiful bird was showing off his amazing feathers in an arch over his head.

He slowly let the fan down behind his gleaming body so that the feathers trailed behind him. Then he raised the fan above his head again. He started to turn in a circle and rattled his feathers at a smaller bird with mainly brown, white and speckled feathers.

We were mesmerised by the performance. The showy bird then strutted slowly away, followed by the smaller bird. We crept silently behind them. They did not seem to have noticed us. Not wanting to tackle the bird with the long tail feathers, we decided that the brown and white bird would make a lovely feast.

They were still absorbed in each other when we pounced on the brown bird. However, we were not prepared for the violent reaction of the male peacock. He attacked us, pecking with his hooked bill and clawing with his powerful feet. Fur and feathers flew and we yelped in pain and surprise. Humans then ran towards us, shouting and waving their arms.

I had endured enough and dashed into the woods. I found a place to lick my wounds and hoped that my brother would find me. Sure enough, he eventually appeared. He was limping and blood was dripping from his jaw. I licked him until the blood stopped. We were unlikely to grapple with peacocks again. We were hurting, miserable and still hungry. Where should we look next?

We followed a gravel track leading to a path at the bottom of a cutting. Suddenly, we were face to face with a strange creature, about the size of the ball we had played with recently.

I sprang forward and closed my jaws around the lumpy animal. Water squirted out of each side of my mouth but I kept biting. It had a strange, acidic taste but at least I felt full again. We hunted around for more so that my brother could also fill his empty stomach. We managed to sniff another out before continuing along the same route. One toad each was quite enough.

Eventually, the path opened out to a wide expanse of hard surface, typical of manmade works. Several birds were pecking at seed and crumbs, scattered over the ground. They ignored us, so we decided to strike. There was confusion as the birds tried to take off while we were amongst them. We grabbed a wing and a leg between us and brought a fat bird to the ground.

Humans started yelling at us, as we had come to expect, so we ran off as well as we could with the bird dangling between us. We did not stop until we reached an earth and boulder patch, where we were hidden from view. Our next meal was much nicer than the watery, squishy toads.

We slept uneasily before heading back towards some distant trees. Hopefully, we could get away from interfering people. We hurried past the pigeons that had returned to their feeding area. There was a whirring of wings as the birds rose into the air at our approach.

I did not recognise the thicket that we now wandered through. It was not as dense as our usual woodland. There was human rubbish dumped everywhere. It was a mess, so we had no intention of staying.

After reaching a small clearing, we sniffed the air, hoping to smell the rich, earthy aroma of home. Nothing was familiar. We circled around and decided to aim for a dense group of trees on the horizon. We avoided contact with other beings.

Our trek took us to the edge of a large pasture. The trees grew beyond a herd of grazing cattle. The late afternoon sunshine made their bracken-coloured coats gleam.

We skirted the rear of the animals, cautiously, and slunk into the woods. Our priority was to look for shelter. We would investigate the farmland the next day. We slept in the shelter of an old shack, close to the cattle.

Early the following morning, we followed the fence that enclosed the pasture. We kept the sun on our backs and soon started to warm up. The bronzed cattle were lying in the field, chewing the cud, but we did not want to attack them. We wanted to explore our new surroundings.

The fence guided us to the right but it was still alongside the wood. Another field lay ahead and it was full of cloud-like creatures. Birds were singing and these animals were bleating. "Baa" could be heard all round the field.

We scrambled over a wooden gate and moved slowly towards the sheep. A little lamb wobbled in front of us while its mother challenged us to come any closer. We defied her and attacked the helpless youngster before she could defend it.

Without hesitation, we dragged the lamb to the gate. My brother clambered over and tugged at the lamb while I shoved its rear end with my front paws. I became aware of the mother rushing at me so I also leapt up and over the gate. We pulled the body into the wood and tucked into breakfast.

When we had eaten as much as we could, we dragged the carcass to the shack and looked for some water. A dew pond in the cattle field was ideal. The area would be perfect as a new home.

The lamb lasted a couple of days. For the first time in a long while, we found time to play. Life felt good again.

Once we were hungry again, we set off from the shack in the opposite direction. There were more fields with different kinds of cattle in them. Some had fearsome-looking, sharp horns on their heads. We would come off badly if we tried to confront them.

We padded on, in the hope of finding more sheep. The next field contained mottled cattle. Some of these were smaller than the horned animals. Should we try killing one of them?

We wriggled under a gate and lay down, studying the black and white calf in front of us. Could we attack and eat something as large as this? Could we stash it away safely?

I was still considering the problems when my brother stood and moved towards the calf.

A loud thwack and crack echoed round the field. The sharp, scary noise bounced back from the trees and hurt my ears. I tried to stand and run away but my brother's limp body fell on top of me. Another shot rang out as I struggled to get up.

Pieces of my brother's fur flew past my nose as I managed to free myself. I dodged the flailing hooves of the panic-stricken calf. In the blink of an eye, I was in the wood and running for my life. Thinking back, the terrified calf must have shielded me from the farmer's aim because no more shots came close to me.

Eventually, I sank into some dense undergrowth, still trembling, shaking and gasping for breath. I stayed hidden and listened intently for any unusual sounds. I hoped that my brother would be able to find me but I never saw him again. I did not really expect to see him because I had come to know the limpness of a dead body.

Chapter 4

Loneliness

I do not recall moving from that spot all day. After a miserable night, I felt thirsty and I ached. I was too unhappy to feel hungry but I needed to check the area for danger and shelter.

My hind leg was sore. As I licked it, I realised that I was spattered with my brother's dried blood. I felt comforted by his taste. Could I survive without him? Did I want to survive without him?

I stood up carefully and looked around. I listened to the sound of birds going about their business. I saw and smelt the blossoms. Yes, I did want to live but I would have to find small prey that I could catch on my own. I would hunt for birds, furry animals and, if necessary, toads.

Limping towards a clearing in which logs were stacked, I had to make a decision. Two trails merged. Which should I take? My brain was only working slowly. I would have to sharpen up if I was to survive.

The rutted tracks ahead of me looked as though they led to humans and I did not want that. I chose the narrow path leading to the right. I was heading into dense forest. That suited me fine.

To start with, I wandered along in a daze not really taking in my surroundings. The blend of earthy fragrances filled my nostrils – decaying leaves, moss, pine needles and peat. The trilling and twitter of many birds, with the occasional mocking cry of woodpeckers, vibrated round my head. I embraced those senses. They would be part of my future. I started to feel better.

With my head held higher now, I trotted along. I glanced left and right and started to sniff the air for food and water. In a damp, dark corner of the forest, I saw some shiny disks on thin tubes. They smelt edible so I took a small bite. One bite led to another and before long I had eaten the whole clump.

I noticed other clusters of fungi in the area so I looked for markers that could lead me back. There was a group of massive trees ahead, far taller than any I had seen before. There was food and some boggy pools of water. If I could find shelter too, it would be a good place to live.

I climbed the slope to my right, looking for a fallen tree or a hole that I could crawl into. I found a couple of possible spots that would do overnight but were not really suitable for a long-term stay. I picked a scrape under a root system and fallen tree trunk. I slunk under the trunk and turned round and round until I felt most comfortable. Then I settled down for the night.

As I peered out of my new den, I started feeling very lonely. I missed my brother. In the gathering gloom, with many unfamiliar sounds and smells around me, I missed the reassurance of his presence. I missed his soft snuffling, woofing and gentle yipping in his sleep. I missed his warm body, rising and falling with his breathing. I missed his companionship and play-fighting, even though he was sometimes a little too rough. Now I would have to make my own choices and catch my own prey. He had been my rock – solid, dependable and reliable.

I was uneasy and restless but dozed off for short periods. At first light, I stretched and shook and clambered down the slope. I could feel bugs in my fur so I had a good scratch. I realised then that I was feeling very hungry indeed.

Remembering the shiny disks, I tried to spot the tall trees. However, it was difficult to make them out from the forest floor. So I scrambled back up the slope. I could see far better from my den and headed off towards the giant redwoods. I started chewing a tuft of fungus. That would do until I could find something meatier.

I picked the biggest tree and worked in increasing circles around its trunk, sniffing the air for food. I soon found that it was hard work running up and down the slopes. So I worked backwards and forwards along the ridge at the top of the steep incline.

There were fewer trees on the ridge and it became rockier. The rocks gave creatures more hidey holes, where I was more likely to find food. There were more flowers and bugs because the sun was not screened by the leafy canopy of the forest, now below me.

As I was nosing around some promising rocks, I spotted a pretty flower - the colour of the sky on a clear day. A couple of spotty insects had landed on the flower head, so I bit it off as a tasty treat.

I could hear movement and the rhythmic sound of grazing. I did not feel alarmed but I looked up at the next ridge to check where the sound was coming from. A brown pony was munching away on the sparse grass on the hill.

It ignored me so I carried on looking for a meal. I found a group of little balls dropped by the furry animals with the short, white tails that they flashed at any sign of danger. I sat and waited by the rabbit midden, keeping still and quiet.

I was beginning to nod off in the warm sunshine when a rabbit flopped down on a grassy patch just to my side. I opened my eyes wide in surprise but only hesitated a moment before leaping onto the unlucky animal's back.

This was my first catch on my own. It reminded me of the first time that my brother and I caught our first meal. I dragged my prize to a gap between the rocks and ate my fill.

Feeling replete and comfortable, with the sun on my black fur, I dropped into a deep sleep. I was vaguely aware of the browsing pony, the buzzing insects and chirruping birds but I was sure I was safe. I was revived.

It was dusk when I woke. Droplets were clinging to my eyebrows and my coat was damp. I stretched and shook vigorously. A shiver ran down my back. I picked up the remains of my kill and looked for a better hole to spend the night. The darkness seemed to last for hours and hours because I was not sleepy. I was alone and friendless.

I spent the following days moving between the ridge and the giant redwood trees. I kept myself busy during the days, hunting for rabbits and returning to the boggy pool to drink. When I could not catch any prey, I returned to the fungus area amongst the trees. I also found a few patches of different kinds of fungus on the grassy outcrops on the ridge. I discovered that one type of fungus made me feel unwell, so I avoided that.

The ponies on the ridge accepted my presence and I enjoyed being near them. They were always calm and spent their days simply cropping the grass and scrub. Sometimes, they nuzzled and blew into each other's noses. When I discovered their dew pond and a long water trough, I no longer had to drink out of the bog.

It was during the night that I felt isolated. The only warm bodies that I could snuggle up to now were those of my occasional, late-evening kills. That was hardly a comfort, other than knowing that I had enough food for the following day. The supply of rabbit supper dried up quickly, however, because they learned how to avoid me.

Birds frantically rearing their young became my main prey, not to mention the fledglings themselves. I know it sounds harsh but I knew of no other way to survive. That was how the spring and summer progressed.

Nowadays, I am well fed by my human companions. I no longer hunt other creatures because I do not need to. I simply admire them and sometimes even protect them from other predators.

As the days grew shorter, the longer nights became more empty and cold. Many flowers died, leaving sweet, juicy berries in the hedgerows. They were a special treat and cheered me up after the lonely darkness.

Humans came to the ridge and led the ponies away. There was very little grass and scrub left for them to eat. My life was more desolate now. I spent more time in the forest, away from the windy ridge.

One consolation was that the squirrels were absorbed in hoarding acorns, sweet chestnuts and pine cone kernels. Before hiding their food stocks, they looked around to make sure that other squirrels were not watching them. However, they did not notice me lurking in the dark shadows.

After a few failed attempts at catching them, I eventually managed to grasp one. I developed a technique for luring them close to me and then lunging at them headlong. To do that, I collected a mouthful of nuts before crouching under the decaying bracken, dropping the nuts in front of my hidden body.

There were more types of fungus around at this time. I only ate those that smelt good but, even so, some gave me tummy upsets or weird dreams. My success at catching squirrels meant that there were fewer for me to eat. The birds were gobbling up the berries as the weather became colder. My food sources were disappearing rapidly.

Storms raged across the forest canopy more often. The wind howled through the trees, driving leaves into swirling clouds and dust squalls into my eyes. The driving rain soaked my fur day after day. I was miserable - alone and miserable. My den was damp, cold and draughty in the long autumn darkness.

My boggy pool covered a vast area now. It became more difficult to find dry tracks to walk along. I spent a great deal of time hunting along the ridge, trying to keep out of the worst of the wetness.

Occasionally, shafts of weak sunshine penetrated the gloom. I would then let the sunbeams warm and dry my back. That felt so good after the weeks of dankness. I soon learned, however, that sunny days led to bitterly cold nights.

Pools iced over and bushes became covered in pretty white spikes. It became more difficult to eat and drink. Even many of the birds left the forest, looking for easier places to forage.

If I was to survive, I would have to leave too. Where could I go? Should I risk begging from humans again? I would have to try. There were usually better places to find shelter near humans.

Feeling anxious, I headed towards the ridge. Humans had taken the ponies away from the rocky ledges so there must be a track in that area. I found a muddy trail, which I began to follow. All the rain had washed away the scent of the ponies but it seemed a good place to start.

I padded along as quietly as I could in case some prey came into view. As usual, I stopped and sniffed the air from time to time. However, the air was cold and still and all smells seemed to be masked. The trail dropped down the hillside. The forest was to my right.

The temperature rose a little and some of the ice melted into droplets. Seeing some berries ahead, I pulled them carefully off a twig which also held spiky leaves. The wet berries helped to quench my thirst.

As I wandered on, I could see that the forest began to peter out. There were thickets and scrubby heath instead. I noticed people with their dogs. Their breath hung on the cold air. I stood and watched, trying to decide whether or not to join them.

They were noisy and excited so I slunk back into the cover of the woodland. I was not yet ready for confrontation. I would try to find a building which I could approach undetected. Then I could scavenge and beg at a time of my choosing.

Although I could still hear the dogs and humans in the distance, the wooded area was silent apart from the drip,

drip of melting hoar frost. I looked for more berries and fungus. I was starving and in need of shelter until I could continue my journey, without being spotted.

After a fruitless search, I flopped down beside an old tree trunk for a rest. A few minutes later, I heard a soft thud followed by the rhythmic rustle of fallen leaves. A blackbird was deftly turning leaf litter, in its own hunt for food. I slowly tensed my muscles and gently lifted from the cold ground. I sprang and caught the bird unawares. I felt better after that.

I continued looking for shelter and water. The light was fading rapidly even though the day was still young. A glimpse of the sky through the tracery of bare branches and twigs above me showed solid, sallow, cloud cover. It seemed ominous to me. Eventually, I found an exposed root system that I could crawl under. I curled up and went to sleep to conserve what little energy I had.

The total silence woke me. It was unnatural. I could not believe my eyes. Everything was coated in a thick, white covering. Even the tree trunks were splattered in the fluffy, white, cloud-like substance.

Sticking my nose into the soft, cold whiteness, I pushed my way out of the shelter. I tried biting the covering but it melted in my mouth and made me sneeze. I leant forward, trying to force a way through, but it would not give. I tried to clamber over the surface but I just sank. Lowering my snout, I ploughed a trench and made some headway.

My efforts warmed me up and I started to enjoy myself. I pranced and rolled around. I slipped and slid and crunched along. It was exciting. My progress was slow and I had no idea where I was going. I could not recognise or smell anything but I did not really care at that moment.

I had made a mess of the covering around the root den. Everywhere else was smooth. Once in a while, a chunk of the soft white stuff dropped from the canopy but did not hurt.

To my surprise, I came across a wide track and decided to follow it. It was bound to lead to humans and, hopefully, food. Lifting my front paws high, I stepped along. Sometimes I sprang and leapt forward. It was very tiring.

Stopping for a rest, I noticed little footprints leading into the trees on both sides. Once my breathing was back to normal, I decided to check out what had made the marks. I scrambled up a bank and into the woodland.

Several of the sets of footprints that I followed just stopped dead. They must have belonged to birds that had flown away. A different set disappeared into a hole in a tree trunk. I sat quietly outside the hole for a while but nothing emerged. A dollop of white stuff landed on my head, dislodged by a bird that started trilling sweetly. It was as if it wanted to share a magic moment in the transformed world.

I realised that the food of all the forest creatures was covered by the white blanket. I was wasting my time there so slid back down to the humans' track. I continued until I reached a pathway that led off to my left. I could see buildings in the distance and hear shouts of joy as young people frolicked in the ground covering.

Even though I approached the buildings cautiously, a dog started barking aggressively to warn me off. It carried on growling after I had gone well past its shelter. The commotion sent a flock of birds into the air behind another house. As I tramped softly towards that dwelling, I noticed that the birds returned to a table on a tall stick. They were pecking at food on the flat surface.

The birds took to the air again as I scrambled over the gate into the yard with the tall table. However, I could not reach the food, even when I stood on my hind legs. I felt the table tilt when I put my paws on the stick.

I leapt up towards the tilted edge and managed to pull it down a little further. I continued pushing on the stick and leaping up at the edge until the table was at such an angle that the food slid off. Bread crusts, nuts and other titbits plopped into the snow. I stuck my muzzle into the snow and gobbled up the lot.

Throughout my antics, the birds scolded me and one even flew at my head. I was ready for it the next time it hurtled towards me. I leapt up at it and caught a wing, pulling the poor creature to the ground. I deftly twisted the feathers off its body and ate it. The hubbub set the angry dog into a rage so I climbed the gate again and wandered on.

Several of the buildings I passed had bird tables in the yards behind them. I was able to raid some of the tables but others were firmly held in place, way out of reach, and I could not budge them. Never mind, I had eaten enough to keep me going for a few more hours.

I was getting close to the children playing in the snow. They were rolling handfuls into balls and throwing them at each other. The youngsters had also made two huge spheres and placed one on top of the other. They had pushed branches into the sides of the lumps. The top ball even looked like a face.

I walked towards the happy group along the wide tracks left by the rolling spheres. Then the young people started throwing some of the snowballs at me. These simply broke into soft pieces when they hit me. I found myself joining in with their game. When I ploughed my head through the snow, they burst into giggles.

I could smell food whenever I was close to the snowman and realised it was the orange nose on the face. So I stood up, seized the nose and crunched it up. The young people rolled around in fits of laughter. One disappeared into the building and quickly returned with a handful of noses. They put one back on the snowman's face but fed the others to me, one by one.

The children made such a fuss of me that I tried to follow them when they all moved towards their doorway. They would not let me in but came out with bowls of meat and water. I decided that I would search for shelter there and explored the buildings.

There were several sheds in the children's yard and these had a canopy above them, linked to the back entrance to their home. I squeezed into a gap between the wooden buildings. That would do for the night. I had been very anxious about meeting humans again but the day had been great fun. I had almost forgotten what fun was.

I was woken by the sound of dripping all around me. The whiteness was disappearing. I stretched and shook myself. My body was aching after being wedged between the sheds overnight.

Wandering to the front of the children's home, I saw that the snowman was standing on a patch of grass. The branches, used to resemble arms, had fallen to the ground. I put my paws on top of the largest sphere and grabbed the nose. I like carrots. Nowadays, I pinch them from my companions' horses.

Water was running off the surfaces that had been coated in white the day before. Pity. It had been beautiful while it lasted. The world had only changed for a short time. However, ribbons of snow still lay along the bottom of hedgerows and in the shadows.

Chapter 5

Companionship

While I was deciding what to do, the children came out of their home and filled up the bowls with food and water again. They chattered happily and stroked my back as I ate. When I had finished, they called to me and encouraged me to follow them.

They headed back down the lane towards the woods. As we approached the last building, the angry dog started barking furiously. The youngsters hesitated, had a chat and then knocked on the door. I stayed in the lane.

A man opened the door, firmly holding on to a rope around the neck of a large, black dog. The children spoke to the man and they all turned round to look at me. The man shook his head and closed the door again, struggling to keep his dog from charging into the lane.

The young people seemed puzzled and headed back to their own home. I followed. A woman appeared as we walked up the path. The children talked to her and they kept looking at me. I sat blinking in the weak sunshine. They ran back towards me and one flung her arms around my neck.

We all danced into the lane again and splashed around in the puddles. We ran up and down together until we were exhausted. The youngsters threw themselves at the snowman and sat on the larger sphere, their backs resting against the smaller lump. I flopped down at their feet, panting.

Once we had all recovered, the children went to the sheds at the back of their home. They tugged a door open and placed some chunks of wood in front of it, to wedge it open. They tried to persuade me to go into the shed but I remembered the time my brother and I had been imprisoned. I sat outside.

One of the children disappeared through the back door and came back with a large covering. She showed it to me then coiled it into a corner of the shed. I stayed where I was. The child curled up on the covering and again tried to persuade me to enter the shed. I continued to sit still.

The boy brought the food and water bowls to the shed, having refilled them. He put them just inside the entrance, to entice me in. They made a fuss of me again and went into their own home, leaving me outside.

I sat and waited until it became obvious that the young people were not coming back that evening. The food was good and afterwards I felt the need for a nap. I cautiously went to the blanket in the corner of the shed and sniffed it. I could smell the child on it. Feeling reassured, I walked round and round on the blanket until I had made a nest. I settled down and eventually fell asleep.

The shed door was still wedged open when I woke up. I lapped at the water bowl then stretched and scratched. I wandered round the buildings. The snowman no longer had a face but the two shrunken spheres still stood on their patch of green. I heard the back door open and I smelt food. I went back to the shed and the boy was filling the bowls again. He patted me but did not stop to play.

Having gulped down the meaty chunks, I returned to the snowman and waited for the youngsters. They seemed subdued when they came out. They were carrying bags and carefully picked their way around the puddles in the lane. There was no running and splashing that day.

I followed them down the lane, which eventually opened out to a smooth wide area of grey with nothing growing on it. The children stood by a post and were joined by others. They kept looking at me and stroking my fur until a long car came along. They all climbed into it but would not let me go with them. I sat and waited for ages but they did not come back.

Eventually, I carried on walking along the grey path in the direction the long car had gone. I felt alarmed as many smaller cars whizzed past me. There was no sign of other humans even though I padded in front of a long row of buildings.

Once the buildings petered out, there were mainly empty fields on both sides of the grey surface. I did not like the stream of cars that ruffled my fur and blew dust into my eyes, so I climbed a gate into one of the fields. Where next?

I did not want to head out over the open countryside. I wanted to find another place where people would feed me and play with me. I could go back to the children's shelter but they did not seem to want me around that day. I decided to walk alongside the hedge that separated me from the rushing traffic.

After covering the length of two fields, I came across a pond. However, I could not drink from it because it was still iced over. I carried on and reached another row of buildings. One had benches and tables outside, beside a car park. It looked promising so I scrambled under a fence and waited by the entrance.

I was becoming very cold when a car drew up and two elderly people struggled to open the door. I followed them into the building, headed straight to a bowl of water and lapped greedily.

One of the people sat at a table close to a pile of logs. There were more logs in a crevice behind a mesh and these were crackling, glowing and giving off heat. I sat between the old lady and the warm logs.

The grey-haired man carried drinks back to the table where they stroked me as they chatted to each other. The man walked back to the long table where he had first picked up the drinks. He spoke to a younger person on the other side of the long table before he came back and sat down.

I felt warmer than I had for months and started to doze until the smell of hot food filled my nostrils. I sat up when I realised that the food was being delivered to the elderly couple's table. I remembered my old trick of glancing from plate to face in the hope of receiving titbits.

It was a while before they took pity on me. Their plates were almost empty when they started to hand me the remaining morsels. However, I had eaten well over the last few days so I was not starving. The humans continued to make a fuss of me while they had another drink.

When they stood up to leave, I decided to follow in the hope of being looked after by them. I slipped out as they grappled with the door again. The people shuffled to their car but shut the doors quickly so that I could not climb in.

Once again, I was out in the cold so toddled round the buildings seeking a warm corner somewhere. There were many outbuildings and I soon found shelter. It was too early to settle down for the night, however, so I went back to the front door in case more people would let me back into the warmth.

Sure enough, another group turned up and I snuck in between them. I headed back to the warm logs and some of the men sat at the table near me. They drank and chatted noisily until their meals turned up. I went from man to man, putting my paws on their knees in turn. Several of them laughed and handed scraps to me. That was the way to beg, I remembered.

They left all too soon and I followed but they chased me away from their cars. I sat by the door again, waiting for my next victim. The next few humans would not let me in even though I tried to slide past them. I was very cold when I eventually managed to squeeze past an elderly woman.

I fell asleep beside the warm logs. When I woke, everyone had gone except the human on the other side of the long table. I finished the water in the bowl and the remaining human topped it up again. She kept talking to me as she moved about. I was happily surprised when she put a bowl of food in front of me. It was a shock later, however, when she opened the door and shoved me outside.

The light was fading so I padded round to the shelter that I had chosen earlier. I made myself comfortable. I was drowsy but not really tired. It took me a while to adjust to the unfamiliar sounds. Once I no longer felt at risk, I slept lightly.

I kept thinking of the strange nature of humans. One minute they were kind and friendly but then they ignored me or turned on me. Where would I find companions that would allow me to stay with them? Perhaps I should go back to the children. I fell asleep thinking of the fun we had had in the snow.

The temperature rose during the night but it became wet and windy. In the morning, I sat outside the doorway to the public house but I became colder and wetter. I whined loudly and scratched at the door but had no reaction. I decided to retrace my steps and go back to the children.

I pushed my way back under the fence and into the field. I stopped for a drink at the pond. All the snow and ice had melted overnight but the wind was now howling across the field, driving stinging shafts of rain into my side.

After passing the post where I had last seen the youngsters, I trotted into the puddle-strewn lane. The remains of the snowman drew me to the shelter of the shed. The door was still wedged open so I shook vigorously before snuggling into the blanket to warm up.

After some time, I thought I could hear children's voices. I wandered into the lane and, sure enough, they were battling against the gale. In my happiness at seeing them again, I hurtled towards them, barking loudly.

I was stopped in my tracks by the sound of my own voice. It was now deep and powerful. The yip and yap of puppyhood had gone. I danced around the youngsters and they laughed, despite getting drenched.

The girl gave me a hug once we were in the shelter by the back door. The boy went inside, returning with bowls of meat and water. My wagging tail splashed them and they shrieked with delight. They disappeared indoors while I tucked into my meal.

It was a while before the back door opened again. A couple of adults stood alongside the youngsters. They were obviously talking about me. The children seemed very subdued.

The woman opened another building and drove a car into the lane. The man rummaged around in that building and came towards me with a length of rope in his hand. The little girl encouraged me to get into the car and the man slid the rope around my neck. He held me firmly while the woman drove the car.

I felt unwell and started retching. The car was swaying violently and I was scared. I did not know what was happening and I could not breathe properly. The man's grip was so strong that I could hardly move.

When the car stopped and the man pushed the door open, I was off. He shouted and started chasing me but I was not stopping for anyone or anything. The rope trailed behind me and sometimes held me back. I just used my terror-fuelled strength to tug myself free each time and kept running.

Once I thought I was far enough away from the man, I checked my surroundings. Why had the children betrayed me? I thought I had found a new home but I would ***not*** be returning to the shed. I would have to find a new shelter.

The weather was getting worse so I cowered behind a large tree, facing a beech hedge. The crispy leaves rustled and whistled in the wind but they gave me some protection. I pawed at the rope around my neck and eventually managed to push it over my ears. I was alone again but at least I was unfettered.

Pushing my way through the hedge, I followed it towards more buildings where I hoped to find somewhere to spend the stormy night. I found a dry corner out of the wind and sank to the ground, feeling miserable. If my memory serves me well, that was when I started gnawing at the fur on my paws. Needless to say, I did not sleep.

Humans could not be trusted but I needed them to provide enough food to get me through cold, wet and stormy days. Every time I thought things were getting better, they suddenly got worse. I seemed to do best at the buildings with outside tables and car parks. The best way of getting into those buildings was by pretending to belong to the customers. I decided to look for another public house.

As I walked away from my overnight shelter, a movement caught my eye. I glanced up at a window to see a handsome cat watching me with disdain. I put my nose into the air and walked away as if I did not care. I shook and scratched when I was out of the cat's line of sight.

I wandered along the line of properties, looking left and right. I spotted some low, bird tables and raided them as I continued my journey. Dogs barked as I passed but I took no notice.

That was the way my days panned out over those dreary months. I became more cunning. My reactions grew swifter and I used humans to get into public houses, where I could scrounge food.

Gradually, the days became longer, the weather generally improved and wildlife returned to the scene. Birds and their young abounded in the gardens and my surroundings started to remind me of the time before my reliance on people. I decided to try and find the woodlands and heath again. The pickings were richer there.

Loping out of a village, I looked for higher ground so that I could find trees with nearby open country. I came to a gate with a glorious view over rolling fields. I decided to aim for the forest on the horizon.

I would not tackle the animals in the fields. That was how I had lost my brother. Instead, I hunted the birds and creatures amongst the trees. I managed to catch enough to survive but I rarely felt full.

I remember a violent storm one night. I had been really scared. I could hear the wind tearing towards me, building to a crescendo, screaming through the tree tops and shredding the leaves from the branches. I had not slept but the next day I was able to feed on the birds that had perished.

A couple of days later, I came across a young stag. It was gorging itself on leaves from a tree that had fallen during the storm. I sank to the ground.

Could I tackle the animal on my own? The nodules on its head were short and looked soft so I did not think they would injure me. It looked as though any flight would be hampered by the toppled tree's branches. I chose to give it a go.

I slunk away so that I was downwind and could creep up behind the deer. The sounds of my stealthy approach were masked by the snapping noises made by the beast itself as it crunched up the twigs and leaves.

I sprang onto some branches and sank my teeth into the animal's neck. It struggled but could not escape from the foliage with me dangling from its neck. Eventually, it succumbed and I feasted for days.

Another encounter I recalled was when I was challenged by a huge, white bird. I had been following a stream on its tumbling journey downhill. There was plenty of prey beside the water so I was not going hungry.

When the bird reached towards me with its rigid, long neck, I tried to grab it. However, it hissed at me fiercely and snapped its beak. It ran at me, flapping its powerful wings. Then it smashed its beak into my brow, neck and side. I yelped in pain and ran off. I always kept clear of swans after that.

The mainly warmer, long days were otherwise uneventful. Life was reasonably comfortable but lonely. I just tried to find enough to eat and make the most of each day. I loved the feeling of sunshine on my black back when I had the chance to rest between hunts. The warmth seemed to ease the aches in my joints.

After a while, however, I noticed that the periods of darkness were lengthening and becoming colder. I had fewer hours to hunt but I was able to feast on squirrels again as they became obsessed with hiding their nuts.

The leaves on the trees were changing colour and berries appeared in the hedgerows again. Some days were glorious but others were wild, windy and miserable. I usually had to eat fruit when the weather was stormy as everything else sheltered. I still enjoyed the juicy sweetness of berries, particularly after chewing fungus.

I started hearing strange, mournful, bellowing sounds. These vibrated throughout the woods but I could not identify them. I decided to investigate by moving cautiously in the direction of one of the many sources.

A large stag with magnificent branches on his head was parading on a grassy knoll ahead. From time to time, he pawed at the ground and sniffed the air. Then he strutted up to a group of does gathering nearby. He drew his breath in over his gums as he passed each female deer.

The stag spotted a rival approaching and rushed at him. He lowered his head so that his antlers challenged the intruder. The antlers of both stags crashed and became entangled. They shoved each other, twisting their antlers to free themselves. Then their headgear clashed again and again as they tried to force each other to give way. I was scared but enthralled by the power of those determined beasts.

While the battle continued, I could hear other stags bellowing. Some of the does slunk away to inspect the alternative suitors. The contrast between the violent behaviour of the stags and the apparent indifference of the does amazed me. I resolved never to go close to agitated stags.

One night, a gale raged and I pushed back as far away from the entrance to my lair as I could get. I could hear the unnerving sound of nuts, acorns, conkers and twigs falling around me. I was reminded of my gloom, months ago, when the weather turned nasty and I had to try to fend for myself.

That was when I decided to seek out humans again. Surely there must be people who were always kind and would be my long-term companions?

There was still enough food around to keep me going but I had an uneasy feeling that it would become more scarce. I found some high ground and scanned the area around me. I could make out some barns in the far distance so made my way towards them. At least I could shelter there, if another storm blew in.

It was several days before I reached the barns because I was not in a hurry. I wanted to check my surroundings from a distance before approaching any human habitation. The barns seemed to be deserted. There were no people or animals around, just rusty old machinery and vehicles.

There was a wide track, however, which would lead me to human activity at some time. I padded along the lane, checking for movement and food. Eventually, I reached more tumbled down buildings but there was still no sign of life.

After clambering over some ivy-covered walls, I found a sheltered nook and settled down for the night. I slept really well that night. It was so peaceful away from the rustling leaves of the woodland and the constant murmuring in the canopy.

I continued along the track at first light and drank rainwater from tractor ruts. I was hungry. I looked around for birds, rabbits and fungi. As I looked up, I realised that I was being watched by a bird with red and white chest feathers.

It bobbed and bowed as it sang the sweetest song. The little bird flitted along the lane ahead of me. I would not be able to sneak up on any prey while the robin stayed just in front.

I found a gap in the hedgerow and pushed through. I decided to walk across the empty, open field. The robin would be unlikely to betray me there. I started stumbling over rutted soil and yelped as I felt a sharp pain in my right paw.

I sank to the ground and realised that I had trodden on a twig covered in piercing thorns. With my mouth and left paw, I managed to pull the sprig off. I was able to chew a couple of thorns out of my right paw but one worked its way deeply into my flesh and I could not bite it out.

While licking my wounds, I caught a scent on the air and tried to identify it. At first I could see nothing but brown earth. Then something in the distance twitched. I could just make out an animal that looked like a large rabbit with black and white ear markings.

As I peered at it, I realised that it was watching me. I started to limp towards the creature but it shot off and I had no hope of catching up. The hare zigzagged over the ploughed ground. I marvelled at the power in its long, back legs.

I stumbled on. My foot really hurt but at least I had shaken off the robin. When I reached the end of the field, I saw that I was on the edge of a heath. I breathed deeply, savouring the peaty aroma. Keeping low, I skirted the gorse bushes and eventually caught a meal.

Then I took the time to check my surroundings and decide where to go. Stretching to look over the gorse, I could just make out some buildings on the horizon. I would strike out in their direction. My dark fur soaked up the warmth from the hazy sun and I felt sore but more positive.

As I limped along a narrow pathway, I looked out for more food. I jumped in surprise when I came across a large stag dozing in the sunshine. He took no notice of me and did not look threatening. I guessed he was recovering from chasing does and other stags. I turned back and found a different trail.

As the heath opened out, I expected to see ponies cropping the meagre grass and scrub. However, there were none around. I could see a road in the distance so I decided to move parallel to it. I had to hobble closer to it as the road twisted and was pinched between a group of trees.

Then I was taken aback by a number of sturdy, short-legged animals with broad snouts. They made grunting, snuffling noises as they gobbled up acorns that were strewn across the road and ground. Saliva hung in frothy strands from the corners of their mouths. ***Yuk!*** They ignored me as they feasted. Squirrels in the trees above were scolding the beasts that were eating their food store.

I thought it was too risky to tackle any of the greedy creatures. I felt that the whole group would turn on me and cover me with their drool. If I found a little one, on its own, I might attack it.

I continued alongside the road and spotted some small, shed-like buildings ahead. I raided a bird table in the garden of one property before settling down to see if there were any people that would make good companions. Nothing happened for a long time until a woman approached on a machine with two wheels. She had hair like the flames in the public house fire.

The woman climbed off her machine and rested it against a tree while she opened a gate and wheeled the machine through. She disappeared down a lane so I struggled over the gate and followed her. I watched her go into a shed and return with a deep bowl. In my mind, she was “Flame”.

From a distance, I saw Flame weave between the wooden buildings and stride down another lane, swinging the bowl gaily by a handle. She scaled another gate, removed something from the bowl, and then shook the bowl. In no time at all, a horse started trotting uphill towards Flame. The horse nuzzled her affectionately then put its nose into the bowl.

While the horse was tucking into the food, she started running her hands over the horse’s body. Flame held what looked like a bundle of short twigs in one hand. She talked softly to the creature and stroked it all over in a firm and rhythmic manner.

The animal seemed to relax at her touch and it occasionally responded by tossing its head and gently snorting. They obviously enjoyed each other's company. I felt envious.

Once the grooming and food were finished, Flame lifted a heavy cover off the fence and strapped it over the horse's back. After breathing into the animal's nostrils, she returned the bowl to the shed. I felt sure that she would make a good companion for me as well but I needed to watch other people before I made my choice.

Wandering between the various buildings in the area, I spotted some birds pecking at the ground. They were making clucking sounds as they worked their way methodically over the ground. I crouched down and moved forward stealthily.

When they had their backs to me, I sprang and caught my next meal. The other birds ran around in terror, flapping and squawking. I carried my prize off to a quiet spot under some shelter, where I spent the night.

The next morning, I was woken by angry, human voices. I went to investigate. Two people were looking at the cockerel feathers scattered around. They did not look very friendly so I slipped away before they spotted me. I headed in the direction of more buildings.

I could hear young voices so I moved towards them. However, when I got close, I realised that they were yelling and screaming at each other. Some were throwing things violently, so I passed them by. I certainly did not want to play with ***them***.

A public house lay ahead of me. I lapped from a water bowl and nosed around, chewing bits of food from the ground. As I hobbled towards the back of the property, a dog started barking and growling. I felt safe enough though because the noise was coming from inside. The uproar got worse and a human came to the nearby door and chased me away.

Further along, there were more buildings in straight lines on both sides of a road. People were wandering in and out of the buildings at random. A lovely aroma wafted towards me so I headed in the direction of the source. The door to the place was open so I wandered in.

A long, glass box in front of me contained several rows of glorious looking, tasty treats. Everything smelt delicious. I sat facing a woman who stood behind the cabinet. I looked from her rose-tinted face to some sausage rolls and back to her dark eyes. She looked surprised and did not move for some moments. Then the woman blinked and her face became stern. She yelled at me before chasing me out of the shop.

Feeling disappointed and hungry, I padded on until I reached the last building in the row. A bicycle leant against the end wall. It looked familiar and smelt of Flame. I could not see her but I sensed her presence, so I sat and waited.

My patience ran out eventually. I decided to retrace my steps and went back to the field where her horse was grazing with a number of others. I found a few food pellets on the ground near the gate. Now that I was away from the pastry shop, I no longer felt hungry. The cockerel I had caught the previous day had been nice and plump. I found a good vantage point in the trees bordering the field and settled down in the hope that my possible companion would appear soon.

Some time later, I heard the sound of happy voices approaching. My muscles grew taut. My target was accompanied by a man. They both carried deep bowls, which they rattled. This time, two horses trotted up the lane and greeted the humans.

Whilst watching the cheerful group, I chewed at my aching right paw. The humans chatted quietly as they groomed the horses. They hoisted turnout rugs over the animals' backs then returned to the sheds with the empty bowls. I decided to stay where I was overnight.

As the weak sun rose, I snaffled up the food pellets left on the ground by the horses. I was still undecided about whether or not I would approach the couple but there was an aura about them that I found alluring.

The humans came back to the field later that morning. They were carrying straps and leather. Once they had removed the rugs, they fitted the straps and leather round the head and back of each horse. Then they climbed onto the leather padding on the animals' backs. The party moved off down the lane and headed towards the heath.

I limped along behind them until I found a spot where I could watch their return. I lay down in the bracken and chewed at my paw until I thought I could hear them. I chose to make my move. You know the rest of that initial face to face encounter.

After that first night beside a wooden building in their lane, I followed the couple around. They put out food and water for me and spoke to me kindly. They also checked that my paw was healing and it was.

I spent the next night on the wooden planking outside their home. The following morning, the couple sat either side of me. They stroked me and murmured soothingly.

The man, whom I thought of as "Grey", put a rope around my neck and carried me to his car. Flame drove the car to the village where the sausage-roll building was. I was terrified. I trembled and whined and felt betrayed.

I was unable to escape when Flame opened the car door. Grey held me firmly and carried me into a building that smelt strongly of other animals. People were sitting in a room, holding on to rabbits, cats, caged birds and other dogs. Eventually, a man in a long, white coat checked me all over while my couple held and comforted me.

Then it was back to the couple's home. To my relief, Grey released me and let me roam around the yard. Flame put out food and water for me and carried a blanket to a sheltered area full of logs.

Grey threw a ball towards me and I instinctively caught it and carried it back to him. Flame sat beside Grey and I sat at their feet while they made a fuss of me. Despite the scare they had given me earlier, I decided that these people would be my companions.

Chapter 6

A Home At Last

Listening to my new companions over the next few days, I realised that they usually called each other “Helen” and “Paul”. Other people seemed to call them by the same names. I had never really thought about names before. There had been very few creatures that I knew well enough to put names to.

I thought of my brother as “Rock”, I suppose. The ponies on the high ridge were “Brownie”, “Shiny” and “White” to my mind. I did not know which one was Shiny and which was White but they were always together, so it did not matter to me.

Now my human friends were calling me “Mojo”. ***Mojo***. I liked the sound of that. I was not so pleased when they soaked me with a jet of cold water after rubbing me all over with a strange-smelling paste. I shook myself vigorously afterwards and they rubbed me down with a soft blanket. I must admit that I felt and smelt better after that.

Helen and Paul acted oddly now when they put my food in a bowl. They would not let me tuck in until they had placed a chunk of strange-tasting meat in my mouth. Then, holding my jaws together, they forced me to swallow the chunk. However, my fur started getting thicker and I started feeling really well. I guess they knew what they were doing.

I was very proud one day when Helen fastened two friendship bands around my neck. She cuddled and stroked me. Now I knew that they wanted me to stay with them. The other dogs that I had seen with humans wore friendship bands. Now I knew that I belonged.

As the weather turned cold and damp, Helen and Paul gave me a cosy bed in their home. At first, I passed water beside my new bed. They scolded me for that. I soon learned that I had to scratch at the door if I wanted to go outside. They made a sand box for me to use as my toilet.

Helen and Paul treated me kindly. They learned that I like carrots when I kept stealing them from the horses. I found out what upset them and tried not to repeat my mistakes. They were most annoyed when I caught birds or rabbits to thank them for my new lifestyle. I found it very difficult to curb my instinct to chase other creatures.

We played fetch and tug and rough and tumble and I helped them with the horses. I usually followed them when they rode over the heath or through the woods. I barked to warn them of any danger, particularly if anyone came to the gate to the yard. I had not been that happy for such a long time. Best of all, I almost always had company.

Helen had a machine which she used to join up pieces of cloth or leather. Sometimes I tried to play tug with the material but that usually made her cross. Helen made coverings for all parts of people's bodies, particularly their legs and feet. When other humans came to her work room for coverings, I barked to warn them not to harm her.

Paul often went away for a few days and nights at a time. I made sure that I stayed on guard then. At other times, he sat at a table in our home in front of a bright light-box. His fingers tapped away at buttons in front of the light-box. If I sat quietly beside him, he tickled me behind my ears.

Towards the end of each day, we looked after the horses. I made sure that I cleared up the food pellets that fell, or were about to fall, from their mouths. Afterwards, we would eat our own meals before cuddling up on a soft, long seat. Helen and Paul would tickle my tummy and I was happy beyond belief.

I was excited one evening when we did not eat after sorting out the horses. Instead, Paul put out a number of bowls of little nibbles and crisps. I was ordered not to touch them. I was tempted by the lovely smells but I obeyed my instructions. He was also cooking in a huge container.

I was beginning to drool so Paul pushed me outside. It was not long before I heard cars and people arriving at the yard gate. I barked furiously. The strangers talked to me and seemed friendly so I wagged my tail but kept on barking.

Paul came out to greet them but then he held my muzzle to stop me barking. Everyone was talking excitedly as we trooped into my home. I expected them to go into Helen's work room but they sat on our cosy seats. They also ate the treats that Paul had put out earlier. However, they made a fuss of me and called me by my name so I did not mind too much.

I barked a couple of times whenever more strangers turned up. It was just as well that I did bark because the new arrivals could not be heard over the noise made by the others. The people were loud but seemed very jolly and enjoyed the food that Paul had made for them. I was allowed some of the warm meat once the humans had eaten their fill.

It was good once the visitors left because I helped clear up the mess. I licked the bowls clean and ate the bits that had been dropped on the carpet and flooring. Paul gave me more of the remaining meat.

When our home was back to normal, Helen and Paul flopped down onto the long seat and I squeezed between them. We all sighed. It had been a pleasant evening but the peace was better. There were similar evenings from time to time but I was always pleased when they were over.

Chapter 7

The Health Scare

I was so glad that I had chosen my companions before the dreary winter had closed in. I had been snug, well fed and comfortably sheltered from the howling gales. The rain had been relentless for some weeks but, eventually, the days were becoming warmer and brighter. Buds started to appear on the trees and the birds became more active.

However, over a couple of days, I felt that a big storm was brewing. I became restless and the horses were very uneasy. The wind strength was increasing and the trees were twisting and bending. Paul and Helen wandered round the yard and field, checking that everything was put into the shed or was securely tied down.

That night was very scary. We could hear waves of raging noise intensifying and curling before tearing round the buildings. The violent gusts screamed at us as they tried to break through the roof, windows and doors. When they failed to rip our home apart, they turned on the trees. We could hear screeching and cracking and massive thuds. I spent the night quivering and trembling in my bed.

The winds were still strong the following morning but the worst of the storm had passed. Somehow, our home had survived unscathed – just. When we went outside, we saw that a swathe had been cut through the trees. The felled trunks all lay in the same direction, as if methodically chopped down by a machine.

Branches and twigs were strewn all round the yard and on the planking around the building. One huge tree had crashed down alongside the house and had cracked into two main pieces. Part of the tree's canopy was resting against one wall. We had had a narrow escape.

Once Helen and Paul had scanned the scene of chaos and devastation, they headed as quickly as they could towards the field. Helen carried a bucket of food pellets and Paul had a bag of tools. I went with them, in case they needed my help.

It was difficult to pick a route through to the field. A couple of the other buildings and fences in the yard had been damaged. Fortunately, the fences round the top end of the field had withstood the storm. However, there was no sign of the horses, so I set off to round them up. They were extremely jittery when I found them lying down in the open at the bottom of the field. I barked at them to send them up to Helen and Paul.

Unfortunately, I stood on something sharp buried in the mud. I yelped in pain. I hobbled behind the horses as they scampered up the field. After being soothed by my companions, the horses champed at the pellets. Reassured, they gradually became more relaxed.

Paul carried on round the field, checking the fences, while I headed back to the yard with Helen. I forgot about my sore paw whilst we tried to clear a pathway through the debris.

The smell of shattered wood was glorious in my nostrils. Helen, Paul and the other humans living nearby helped to clear up the mess. The sound of sawing could be heard all around for days.

After the initial excitement and exhilaration in the aftermath of the storm, I started to feel unwell. My injured pad was raw and swollen and I kept being sick. I had no energy and I felt as if I was spinning round and round. Even when I tried to lap up some water, I was sick.

My companions were concerned. I could hear them gently talking whilst stroking me. I tried to wag my tail but it just flopped back onto my bed. I was aware of Paul scooping up my bed with me still in it. Then he supported my lolling head as Helen drove slowly out of the yard. The motion made me retch again.

Was that how my mother felt before she died? I did ***not*** want to die. I was still young and had so much to live for – an exciting home, wonderful companions, regular meals and carrots on demand.

The next thing I remember was the man in the white coat again. I was aware of strange sounds and smells as I came round but I could not move. I seemed to be in a cage and had a tube stuck down my throat. Whiteness floated in front of my eyes briefly before I drifted off to sleep again.

The next time that I woke up, I was feeling much better. My sore paw was wrapped in cloth and my throat hurt but the tube had gone. I scrabbled into a seated position and looked around.

Other dogs were in similar cages and they all seemed poorly. Some had odd cones around their heads. I lapped gently from the water bowl in my cage. To my relief, I managed to keep the water down. It soothed my sore throat.

Before long, a woman in a white coat came into the room. She spoke softly to me as she opened my cage. I staggered out on wobbly legs as she encouraged me to walk around the room. She praised my efforts and stroked me before leading me back to the cage.

Where were Helen and Paul? Would they take me home again or did I have to stay there amongst all that sadness? The woman came back with a little soft meat. She held my muzzle after putting a piece of food in my mouth. I swallowed, remembering what Paul and Helen had done before each meal after my last visit to the people in white coats.

I had to endure a couple more periods of darkness before I was led from the cage into a different room. As I limped between the rooms, I caught a familiar scent on the air. As the door opened, Helen and Paul came towards me with their arms open. I whimpered in delight and wagged my tail wildly. They had come to take me home. I was so happy that I forgot my dislike of the car journey.

What a joy it was to inspect every corner of the yard and our home! All the shattered trees had been cut up and stacked in neat log piles. The storm damage had all been fixed. That lovely smell of newly cut wood still hung on the air though. It was good to be back but I felt tired again.

I fell asleep on our long, soft seat between Helen and Paul as they tickled my tummy and talked quietly to me. I now felt that I could trust people again.

I still had to swallow the horrid chunks before I could tuck into my meals. However, I now understood that my condition would keep improving if I continued to put up with them. It was some time before I had the energy to help with the horses or go on long walks.

Eventually, I was back to my old self. Life was back to normal and I was content. I even overcame my fear of car travel. If I looked out of the car windows at something in the distance, I could cope with the motion. Best of all, my companions were more caring than ever.

My story goes on. I cannot imagine that it can get any better. I no longer chew at the fur on my paws because I am content. I know that I have done some bad things in the past but I did not know of any other way. I had a strong desire to survive. Now that I no longer need to hunt wildlife and birds, I can enjoy watching and listening to them. It is good to be alive and amongst friends.

If you are in a dark place at the moment, have hope. You too could find happiness and contentment. Although harsh at times, life can be wonderful.

The end

ABOUT THE AUTHOR

Margaret Gray loves to be beside, on or under the sea. She also enjoys walking in the countryside and always takes a camera with her. In the past, she has had articles published in diving magazines but always intended to write stories for children after her retirement from public sector administration and finance.

Margaret retired in 2006 to look after her frail in-laws. Sadly, her father-in-law died while she was working her notice. However, she looked after her mother-in-law for eight months, until her mother-in-law chose to go into a home.

During that period, Margaret needed an outlet for her anxiety and frustration. That was when she started "A Tale For All Seasons", a story about a year in the garden of a robin and a blackbird and their relationship with the elderly woman who looks after the garden. It was some time after her mother-in-law's death before Margaret felt able to complete the tale.

With her second illustrated story, "Cuddles The Cuttlefish", Margaret hopes to inspire young people to take an interest in the marine environment. She wants to share her joy in the beauty that can be found underwater. The tale follows the development and encounters of a young cuttlefish. Margaret took the pictures in the waters off the south west coast of England.

"Wilf The Water Nymph", which describes the meeting and budding friendship between a naughty water nymph and a boy, is her third illustrated story. The boy, who calls himself 'Deano', and Wilf learn from each other as the boy helps the nymph to return home. They have several adventures along the way.

After being given two, toy ducks, Margaret wrote about "The Adventures Of Splish And Splosh". A pair of little, plastic ducks are washed up on a Cornish beach, following a shipwreck. They are found by a couple of divers, who take them on a boat-diving weekend. Splish and Splosh are eventually returned to Cornwall in the south west of England. "Splish and Splosh Have More Adventures" is the sequel to this story.

"Dawn Black – Storm Child", is about the short life of Dawn Black, a child born and raised on farms in Cornwall. Dawn overcomes adversity and has a mainly happy life but, sadly, she dies in an accident following a row with a jealous rival.

"Mojo's Story" is about a dog born in the New Forest, in the south of England, after her mother had been abandoned. Only two puppies survived the first couple of months – Mojo and her older brother. Their mother developed a fatal disease, leaving the two puppies to fend for themselves. The tale describes Mojo's struggle to survive, her adventures along the way and how she adopted her human companions. Mojo chose her human friends well and lived a long, happy and contented life with them.

"Olive The Knitted Octopus" describes the transformation in her life once she is spotted by baby Saffron. Olive had spent much of her life sitting on top of a cake tin above a kitchen cabinet. It was not much of a life until Saffron introduced the knitted octopus to all sorts of toys, games and places. As Saffron grew, the adventures and games became more exciting. However, on her first visit to Cornwall, Saffron left Olive on some rocks. The rising tide claimed the knitted octopus and introduced her to the underwater world. The child is later reunited with Olive and they have more adventures, this time above the water.

"The Key To 'Pandora'" is a story about pirates. A couple of young cousins occasionally visit their grandparents' home where they pretend to be pirates. Their grandfather has converted his shed into a pirate ship, called "Pandora" because of all the evil deeds that the ruffians act out in and around the shed. Most of all, the pillagers crave treasure. One spring, the boys' grandfather takes them to Cornwall on their first camping trip. The pirate games and adventures continue on the holiday but the youngsters find a new kind of treasure. The "freebooters", as they call themselves, have an exciting time and build wonderful memories. They look forward to another camping holiday with their grandfather.

Printed in Great Britain
by Amazon

65759325R00054